To my little Molly
—E.S.K.

To Patrick and the beautiful princesses:
A, E, E, J, M, and baby Sophie
—P.S.-P.

Acknowledgments
Pamela and Emily thank our brilliant editor, Mallory Loehr;
our wonderful art director, Jan Gerardi; and our heroic agent,
John Diamond, for enabling us to work together
on this happy fairy tale.

Text copyright © 2003 by Emily Snowell Keller and Pamela Silin-Palmer
Illustrations copyright © 2003 by Pamela Silin-Palmer
All rights reserved under International and Pan-American Copyright Conventions.
Published in the United States by Random House Children's Books, a division of
Random House, Inc., New York, and simultaneously in Canada
by Random House of Canada Limited, Toronto.

www.randomhouse.com/kids

Library of Congress Cataloging-in-Publication Data

Keller, Emily Snowell. Sleeping Bunny / retold by Emily Snowell Keller;
paintings by Pamela Silin-Palmer.
p.   cm.
Summary: A curse by an angry fairy puts a bunny princess
to sleep for a hundred years.
ISBN 0-375-81541-4 (trade) — ISBN 0-375-91541-9 (lib. bdg.)
[1. Fairy tales. 2. Folklore.] I. Silin-Palmer, Pamela. II. Sleeping Beauty. English. III. Title.
PZ8.K355 Le 2003   398.2   2001041750

First Edition

PRINTED IN HONG KONG   January 2003   10 9 8 7 6 5 4 3 2 1

RANDOM HOUSE and colophon are registered trademarks of Random House, Inc.

Sleeping Bunny

Retold by Emily Snowell Keller

Paintings by Pamela Silin-Palmer

Random House 🏠 New York

nce upon a time, there lived a kindly Rabbit King and his Queen. Only one thing was missing from their perfect lives—a baby bunny (which was highly unusual in their family!).

One autumn day in the castle gardens, the Queen burst into tears. "If only I had my own baby bunny to love, I would be the happiest Queen in the world."

In a twinkling, a smartly dressed frog appeared before her. "Your wish shall be granted!" he proclaimed. "A daughter will be born to you before the year is over!"

Sure enough, within a year, the King and Queen had a beautiful baby girl. They named her Princess Bunny and loved her from the tips of her silky ears to the ends of her dainty white paws. To share their joy with the whole kingdom, they planned a great feast. Everyone would be invited, including the eight fairies of the land. The King and Queen knew the fairies would bless Princess Bunny with good wishes for a happy life. However, inviting all the fairies was not as easy as it seemed, for there were only seven golden plates. (Fairies cannot possibly eat off ordinary china!) Thus, only seven fairies were invited. Mildew, the eighth and crankiest fairy, was left out.

CARPE CAROTAE

Mustard Seed:
Spirit

Acorn:
Strength

Cornflower:
Common Sense

Sunflower:
Warmth

Poppy:
Humor

Foxglove:
Kindness

Primrose . . .

The celebration was joyful! Each guest gave Princess Bunny a special present. Then the fairies bestowed their magic gifts. . . .

ut before the seventh fairy, Primrose, could give her blessing, Mildew arrived on a blast of lightning! Furious at having been left out, the eighth fairy pointed a bony claw at Princess Bunny and screeched: "When this bunny turns fifteen, she shall prick her finger on a spindle and die!" Then, with a glare at the horrified guests, she vanished in a whirlwind.

The King and Queen gathered Princess Bunny up in their arms. As they wept, the fairy Primrose floated forward.

"Please don't cry," she said. "I have yet to give Bunny my gift. I cannot undo Mildew's spell, but I *can* alter it. The Princess will indeed prick herself as foretold, but she will not die. Instead, she will fall asleep for one hundred years!" Primrose waved her sparkly wand over the baby.

The King and Queen thanked the kind fairy, but they wondered if sleeping for one hundred years was any better than death.

"We must do all we can to protect Bunny," declared the Queen.

So every spindle in the realm was destroyed.

Time passed, and as the Princess grew, the fairies' blessings were realized. She was smart, strong, warm, witty, and naturally beautiful. Her kindness and generosity made her the land's most beloved rabbit.

On the Princess's fifteenth birthday, her parents sighed with relief: there was not a spindle in sight! To celebrate, they held a birthday ball in her honor.

During the festivities, Princess Bunny felt restless and wandered off to explore the castle. She hopped here and there until she poked her pink nose around a corner and found a dusty staircase she had never seen before. At the top was a curious door with rusted hinges. A golden key was in the lock.

The key turned easily. The door opened. Inside was a tiny room filled with piles of unspun wool and spools of colored thread. A strange old rat was working busily at her spinning wheel.

"Excuse me," Princess Bunny said shyly. "What are you doing?"

"I'm spinning thread from wool, Princess." The old rat grinned, showing her pointy teeth. "Would you like to try?"

Bunny was entranced by the whirling wheel and the rainbow-colored thread. "Oh yes, please," she said, "if you don't mind!"

Eagerly, Princess Bunny reached out to touch the spindle and . . .

. . . she pricked her paw.
With a sigh, Princess Bunny collapsed
onto a pile of wool in a deep, deep sleep.

The moment Bunny closed her eyes, so did everyone else. In the great hall, the King and Queen, guests and servants all fell asleep. Cooks snored among the vegetables. Musicians dreamed over their instruments. Even the breezes stopped blowing as the entire castle fell into an enchanted sleep.

The years passed. An enormous hedge of thorns grew up around the castle, so high and thick that in time it covered even the tallest towers.

The legend of the beautiful Princess who lay sleeping within its hidden halls was passed on for generations throughout the land. Everyone referred to her as the Sleeping Bunny.

Over the years, noble knights tried to break through the tangled thicket in search of the castle and the sleeping Princess, but none succeeded. Each time a brave knight ventured forth, the piercing thorns grabbed him and he was lost forever.

One day a young Rabbit Prince was seeking adventure when he came across an elderly peasant. The peasant told him the story of the sleeping Princess hidden behind a wall of thorns and of the many princes and knights who had disappeared trying to reach her. Bewitched by the idea of finding the legendary Bunny, the Prince searched the land, finally coming upon the enormous thorn hedge. Valiantly, he charged into it with his sword raised . . .

. . . but lo and behold, the thorns parted before him!
As luck would have it, exactly one hundred years had
passed since Bunny's enchantment!

The Prince bounded, heart pounding, through
the open hedge and into the castle. There he
discovered everyone alive yet sound asleep. No
one stirred as he hopped from room to room,
seeking the fabled Sleeping Bunny.

At last he came upon the same winding staircase Bunny had climbed so long ago. He pushed open the door at the top and there, dreaming peacefully, lay the most beautiful creature he had ever beheld. The adoring Prince knelt and kissed her soft, furry cheek.

TEMR BON

Sleeping Bunny's eyes fluttered open.

"Fear not, fair Princess," said the Prince. "You have been asleep for one hundred years. It's time to get up!"

Sleeping Bunny stretched and wiggled her long ears. She looked curiously at the Prince. "Really?" she said. "It feels like I just took a nap."

"Come, I will show you!" said the Prince.

Together they hopped down the stairs. Everything was as before: Music played, vegetables roasted, and breezes blew the sweet smell of roses from the gardens. Just then the fairy Primrose appeared and led Bunny and the Prince to the King and Queen.

"Mildew's curse came true," Primrose announced. "But instead of putting just Bunny to sleep for a hundred years, I put *everyone* to sleep, so you could all wake up together!"

With tears of joy, the King and Queen hugged their daughter and the smiling Prince.

And so the King and Queen ruled once more over their kingdom. Princess Bunny and her Prince grew to truly love each other and eventually decided to marry.

A jolly feast was held in honor of their wedding. This time *all* the fairies were invited. Even so, when old Mildew flew in, a chill descended as she pointed her claw at the bride.

"You must never make the same mistake as your parents!" she cackled gleefully. With that, a magnificent set of *eight* golden plates appeared at Bunny's feet.

Thus it was that everyone lived *hop*pily ever after.